Papers through the Hollows

Liam Adams

Cover illustration by

Liam Adams

Papers through the Hollows
by Liam Adams

We think this book is mostly suited to young adults, aged from 10-12 onwards, although older adults may enjoy it as much!

This book is sold on the understanding that it is the work of a person with intellectual disability and Autism. All creativity is from the author and the text has been edited by his mother to the best of her ability. However, it is understood that the writing may be different from that expected in a formally published novel.

Liam hopes you enjoy reading his book as much as he enjoyed writing it. He would love to hear your feedback; if you wish to contact him his email address is ltahm@icloud.com

July 2022
Revised Edition: January 2026

ISBN: 978-0-6455970-8-0

Papers through the Hollows
Table of Contents

1. The Lost Papers

It was the Age of the Last Time Zone in the Distant Future - or The End of the Line if you want to see it that way. Here, every star was gone and dusted. No more life; no Wi-fi; no planets; no spark. Welcome to the End of Time itself.

Humanity couldn't last as everything was collapsing in from each other and hope of life was dim. Nothing could survive, not even stars or suns.

Open and clear space was all that remained, except for one last thing. Floating in nothingness there was a building cube that had four markings like an 'X' on each side, each of which burrowed down into a small hole. Inside each hole was a path to an incredible, massive, and solitary Library.

This Library contained all the knowledge of humanity that ever existed. It had the most important history books from all the billions of decades of humankind. People thought that if they sent this Library into the future, and if there was any creature left in the cosmos, they would know they were not alone and learn about the mind-blowing heritage that humanity had created.

Now, it would seem that if there was a floating Library that had the most important books ever, there would have to be someone to look after it in case something happened? Yes, if there's a Library, there must always be a Librarian. Well, you could say this librarian is the "LAST" remaining life left. It seemed to this librarian that becoming the "LAST" remaining life was an offer too good to refuse. So he accepted this post. The Librarian wore a red robe with yellow and green lines streaming downwards while being next to each other, the uniform of the Last Court of Loyal Librarians. And now he was indeed the "LAST" Librarian: and his name was Floyd.

Don't let the word "LAST" disturb you in any way; Floyd always took good care of himself. He also wore some slip-on shoes because nobody could tell him to "Take them off!" or "This is the last remaining Library! How dare you wear them in here?!"

He was a 30-year-old man. He was in his early 20s when he decided to take the offer to head into the nothingness and guard this Library at all costs. He studied everything at the academy, so he had everything he needed to know and all the things he needed to live. It seemed Humanity's reservoir was in safe hands.

With all these years of checking the books and guarding the entire Library, Floyd must have had some other things to do in the nothingness? Well, he did have a few hobbies of his own. He played a few of his instruments, or at least tried to play. Most days he spent time reading books by some of the people who have lived. The Librarian thought that this was the time when he felt most human again, and experienced real happiness.

Maybe it was against the rules, but who was there to judge?

At some point this day, Floyd wandered along to his own massive Electronic Organ. It was in a corridor. The Electronic Organ was so huge its keyboard sat on a balcony, beneath which was the large hall.

The Librarian entered and thought he would like to play a tune on the Organ. He walked up to the balcony and looked at the keys as his fingers tingled in the air. He pressed a key and just then, out of nowhere, horns blared, scaring the living daylights out of him. He jumped back in fright.

The Librarian could not believe it: someone was coming towards him through a mist. "BOO!" it cried out in some sort of robotic voice.

It was a robot, running towards the Librarian! The robot had an orb head that was aiming a small circle ball at him like a camera zooming in. It had a metal silver and gold body made by an odd compilation of weird gear. Its voice was a little rusty and indeed robotic. His name was LO-NO, an annoying and misfit robot that the Last of Humanity sent to the Library. His purpose as the "LAST" robot from existence, was to update any news to the Library and to help the Librarian do his job. It appeared that his job was also to make the Librarian's life a whole lot harder!

"LO-NO?" questioned Floyd, startled by the Robot.

"I COULD HEAR YOU COMING IN HERE, SO I PLANNED TO RUN UP AND SCARE YOU!" LO-NO said, chuckling.

"Well, nice try" Floyd told his accomplished robot, pretending LO-NO's plan failed, "but it would seem someone got to it before you" he said, referring to the loud horns.

"I'VE BEEN DOWNLOADING A FEW TUNES WHILE I'VE BEEN POWERED DOWN" LO-NO acknowledged.

"So, you have been doing this stuff while you're off duty?" asked Floyd.

"HEY! EVEN A ROBO GUY NEEDS A LIFE YOU KNOW!"

"Of course, you do" Floyd replied, trying to be comforting, "Remember the point of robotic life was ultimately to explore the meaning of life".

"HA, HA!" LO-NO laughed, "THAT'S WHAT ALL YOU HUMANS SAY, ISN'T IT?" He ran off and left the Librarian alone.

Besides the robot, Floyd had not seen anyone for quite a while. He wished he could meet someone like himself again, or someone who knew how to play the Organ at least.

******

On the 22nd of April 2016 on the planet known as Earth, in the middle of a Science class at Hula College, Professor Rachial was teaching about the Milky Way and how humans may not be alone.

Professor Rachial had long hair and round glasses. She was quite young for a teacher and was proud to be part of the College's society. She knew about everything to do with the galaxy, and the cosmos.

"For every star, there will be another planet in a solar system" she explained, as she was writing on the chalk board, "like ours; there maybe be life, which may be trying to find our planet, just like how we're trying to find more life. Who can tell me which are our closest solar systems?"

She dropped her chalk on the table and waited for an answer from any of her students.

It was a big classroom. It was one of those where the seats were higher in each row. There were about 30 students attending the class, but the room was bigger for more.

"Anyone?" she asks her students, "Anyone? No one knows?"

The students were afraid to put their hands up in case the others thought they were some kind of super nerd.

"No?" she said, disappointed, "well that is a bit disappointing. I would have thought Monkeys flew airplanes instead." She smirked at the board and smiled as she turned around to her students, "Well that will be your homework. We'll see how you go after the holidays".

The students started to get up and walk out of the classroom as the school bell rang. They packed their homework, notebooks, and pens into their bags as they left.

One student was named Jack. He had brown curvy hair and wore glasses; he had a yellow buttoned up shirt and jeans, and those daggy slip-on shoes that teens wore at the time.

Jack was heading out of the classroom and into the school hall. It was a clean hall with lockers and had a black and white shiny floor. He saw his friend Vicky near the corner of the door as he walked out. She had a brown hair as well, with a ponytail; and she wore a black shirt and a white skirt. She was smiling at him as she was waited for him.

"Vick?" Jack said, "why are you waiting out here?"

Vicky was pacing up and down as she came a bit closer to Jack, "Ooh, I was thinking that we could have lunch tomorrow?"

Jack and Vicky were very close friends. They normally saw each other both at school and out of school. They may be called best friends.

"Really?" Jack asked, "right after your science class with Professor Rachial?"

"I thought it was worth a shot" she said raising her head, "Let me guess, she talked about the solar system, and how we could not be alone and all that".

"You know she talks about some very interesting facts and theories, right?" Jack remarked, quite a bit fascinated. Jack didn't actually believe everything about what may be out there in the universe and whether they were alone or not. But he was afraid that one day the universe would revolt, and everything would fly into his face.

"Anyway, when tomorrow?"

"12 o'clock" Vicky suggested "if that's OK with you?"

Jack thought about it for a moment, "Yeah" he said, as he scratched his hair, "that's cool, I don't really have anything on anyway".

"A bit lame I'll say" Vicky said quietly to herself.

"What?"

"Nothing!" she said with a smile, "Cool, I'll see you tomorrow" she replied, as she turned her back and walked down the hall.

"See ya" Jack called back.

As they said goodbye to each other, it was just another normal day for two regular teenagers at school.

******

The Librarian entered the main Library. It was as big a room as you can imagine. The room needed to store everything from the millennia of time. It had the same red carpet as everywhere in the entire Library, but there was some shiny gold floor as it reached the shelves, and the walls were gold as well.

You must wonder what the builders were thinking to build such a sculptured place that used every precious resource in existence. It was as impressive a room as you could imagine but it also had a particular familiarity, like the other more homy rooms in the library. Very strange.

As Floyd arrived in the room, he noticed, up in the air, a few papers were falling from the high ceiling. To Floyd, it looked like maybe the Library was raining papers. Then the first papers flew away on a breeze, just as other papers floated in Floyd's direction.

To his alarm, Floyd saw that in the distance there was not only more papers coming his way, but a yellow, glowing crack through the floor with shiny lights popping out. The floor was shimmering with floating books. It was the pages of these books that were being ripped and flung through the room.

Floyd understood what this was. This was not an unfortunate accident or a pathetic prank by

LO-NO where he should have known better; this was a *hollow*! A *hollow* through time and space! Floyd knew that if these papers flew into the *hollow*, they may be lost forever!

Floyd had only read about what the *hollows* were. Scientists had discovered *hollows* during the thirtieth Century. They were vortex portals that allowed some kind of inter-dimensional travel through space, time or somewhere really random.

Hollows don't have a specific reason for where they go or where they'll end up. They are unlike other space phenomenon; you can't tell where they are going to strike.

Floyd didn't know why the *hollows* ended up at his Library, but he knew that if they were active, it could cause massive trouble.

Floyd ran down the stairs and tried to stop the *hollow* beneath him. Papers flew into his face on the way down causing him to trip down the stairs.

"Ow" he called out as he kept on tripping down, "Ow, ahh! Ow!"

He bumped down to the bottom of the stairs. He saw *hollows* opening and closing as the papers flew through. Floyd watched in horror as this timeless information that held the universe together got lost.

You may be asking, why are these simple boring and stupid books important? They might not be very relevant to use today, but to Floyd it meant everything.

The Librarians and even all of humanity wanted their research and their history to be remembered. But losing about ninety-six percent of it would have triggered the authors to return from their graves and hunt Floyd in his nightmares for the rest of his existence.

Floyd was like a hopeless Librarian on the floor, just watching the papers fly over and over in the room in different directions. Floyd needed to do something, to stop this before it got out of hand. Floyd crawled over to one of the *hollows* as a new army of pages flew above him. He marched like a soldier in the dirt in a warzone; or instead, the o-zone. He needed to close the *hollows*. He was hoping that if he could close them, they might stop dragging papers. He thought it was worth a shot, so he crept along the floor, and aimed toward the front of one glowing *hollow*. He grabbed the two corners of the *hollow* with his hands and pulled it strongly together. Even though grabbing space phenomenon that are made entirely of particles is crazy, just wait till you try it before you can imagine how difficult it is.

Floyd planned to put the two corners of the *hollow* together as it shined fiercely while closing. Floyd tried shutting his eyes because it was so bright, but it was too strong. Floyd tried to close it as tight as possible, as tricky as it was. Finally, the *hollow* was closed, and no other pieces of *hollows* appeared. The remaining papers stopped floating as they slowly fell from the air.

Floyd breathed heavily as he closed the *hollow*. Now closing the *hollows* was the least part of his worries. He needed to find the lost papers that pulled existence together. The *hollows* had taken the last pages of humanity!

2. Back in The Day

It was bad; it was very bad. Pretty bad in fact! If one small piece of any book got lost in any way, it will not just be lost, the entire history it contained would be forgotten, and pieces of the universe would start to collapse.

Thankfully, Floyd knew what papers were missing; it didn't mean he read every book, as he didn't really have the time yet to cover all books. But he was observant, so he could tell where pages were missing, and where they were intact.

There was no one who could punish Floyd for failing the one thing in his job that mattered! – the safety of precious information. But Floyd felt gutted about the *hollow* disaster and was determined to do what he could to fix it.

LO-NO rushed to the Library when he discovered the accident. Floyd told him everything, trying not to hide anything. LO-NO was not happy to hear the news, so he completely flipped out on Floyd.

"HOW COULD YOU LET THIS HAPPEN?!" he cried, in shock and anger at the Librarian.

Floyd had a very guilty face with desperate eyes looking at the robot. "Sorry" he said.

LO-NO didn't have a face, but he tried to give an angry look at Floyd, "YOU LET THIS HAPPEN!!!"

"I didn't!" Floyd argued, "Well…not all of it".

LO-NO was out of patience, "HOW MANY PAGES?"

"I don't know" Floyd cried, "Maybe, a lot?"

"A LOT?" LO-NO pondered deeply, wondering if things were as bad as they seemed, "IF THE LAST HUMANS WERE HERE, THEY WOULD THROW YOU OUT OF THE AIR LOCK IN THIS LIBRARY LIKE ALL THE OTHER LIBRARIANS WHO FAILED THEIR JOBS!"

"Did they?" Floyd asked, concerned.

"DON'T KNOW, ASK THE DEAD" snapped LO-NO.

Floyd rubbed his face, while LO-NO paced up and down the carpet hallway, next to the Library where the accident happened.

"What am I going to do?" Floyd pleaded, as he had no idea what to do.

"DON'T ASK ME!" said LO-NO, who didn't want to assist Floyd's mistakes. "I HAVE NO WAY TO FIND EVERY PAGE THAT SWEPT THROUGH THE HOLLOWS OF THE UNKNOWN!"

Floyd wasn't a coward of any sorts, not like the Librarians before him. He was born for this! His courage welled up inside him and suddenly he called out "That's it!" he had an idea spark, "that's it!"

"WHAT? WHAT?" LO-NO asked, wanting to know his plan.

"If I travel through one of the *hollows*, I could trace it's trail and catch up with it," said Floyd.

"SO, LIKE A PIGGY-BACK?" asked LO-NO.

"Precisely" said Floyd, as if it was a perfect example. "If I could use one of those Trans-Mats that they gave me…"

"*TRANS-MAT*?" exclaimed LO-NO, who had no ideas what it was.

"A traveling device that I could go through" explained Floyd as he stood up, "not only through time and space, no, no, no, but through different dimensions, *hollows*, cosmos, you name it. And even other paths science did not discover."

"SO, IT'S AN INFINITY SPACE HOPPERPIGGY-BACK" said LO-NO.

"Pretty much," answered Floyd, "but like I was saying, if I could follow the *hollow* to where it was heading, I could grab and pick up the papers inside it, and hopefully find the others and come back here before you could say Ah-choo."

"AH-CHOO?" LO-NO asked.

"Never mind" Floyd groaned.

"AND YOU CAN STUDY MORE ABOUT THIS ACCIDENT" said LO-NO, who was coming to understand Floyd's plan.

******

It was Earth, 23rd April 2016, the day after the big school workout and the beginning of the Chillax days to come. It was almost twelve noon, and the sun was still shining for a brand-new day. Jack was at Vicky's house. It was an apartment building at an angle to the street where two roads passed around it. There wasn't really a road; it was one of those pavements where people can walk freely around and don't get run over.

Jack was wearing the same casual clothes from the other day. Vicky opened the door and stepped out. She wore casual clothes too, but with a purple jumper this time. "Are you ready Jack?" she asks him.

"Yeah" he responds as they walk through town.

Jack and Vicky walk to a street a couple of miles away. There were cafes, restaurants, and local shops in the area, but not many houses. They reached the place they were going to have lunch -a restaurant called "Chickee's Chicken". A dumb name it certainly was; it would have been smarter for the business if a more personal name was chosen by the family. But it was, in fact, a delicious restaurant.

The restaurant was at an open space near the alleyway of the street. There were a few people having their meals, and waiters were coming by taking orders.

"So, I'm happy you chose this place" said Vicky, who was enjoying wondering the street.

Jack nodded his head, "Yeah, I normally walk by this area" he said.

"Seriously?" questioned Vicky, who didn't know Jack came by here.

"I've been curious about the menu here" mused Jack, looking at the specials, "but, hey, I don't know what the food is like.".

"You want to?" Vicky asked.

Jack really didn't mind but said "Yeah" as he wasn't sure.

There was a waiter walking up to them. He was wearing casual waiter clothes. He was part of the family business, "Can I get you anything?"

"uhh…" said Jack, who still couldn't decide what to eat, "I think we'll need more time."

The date was going very well. They already had a chat on the way, and they were enjoying themselves. They had a good friendship: Jack and Vicky saw each other after school and helped each other with their homework. Jack liked Vicky, and I mean *really* liked her. There was something really good going on here.

******

Floyd was all strapped in and already to go. LO-NO gave Floyd a dimensional *hollow* device just in case. If Floyd encountered anything unusual or bizarre, he could use it and close the *hollow*. Floyd was pacing and breathing heavily as he had not done anything like this in his entire life.

"OK, WHEN YOU HEAD OFF" said LO-NO, as he was getting Floyd prepared, "THIS DEVICE CAN TAKE YOU BACK AT ANY TIME".

It was a strange looking device. It showed three lines as it moved from left to right: purple, yellow-ish green and black. It also had a wonky arrow to point to where the heck he was or where he was going. There was also a button for him to press, which had an uncertain purpose.

"Thanks" Floyd said, not fond of this device, "Where shall I go? When shall I see you again?"

"DEPENDS" said LO-NO, "I'LL HELP YOU WHEN YOU NEED ME, OR, WELL, NOT"

Then LO-NO jolted his robotic mind and remembered to rush behind Floyd and put the Trans-mat at Floyd's feet. LO-NO then ran over to a lever switch for him to flip. He looked right at Floyd and reminded him of his mission, "YOU KNOW WHAT TO DO! FIND THE PAPERS AND BRING THEM BACK!"

As LO-NO flipped the switch, the black mat turned to white. The white light swung up to the surface and surrounded Floyd as he dispersed into space.

"I'll tr…" he cried as he dissolved.

When Floyd was gone and the trans-mat was off, LO-NO cleaned his hands in relief that the Librarian was gone.

"AHH" he sighed with peace, "NOW, WITH HIM OUT OF THE WAY, WHAT WAS I PLANNING TO DO?"

3. An Unexpected Date

Jack and Vicky were having a great day. They finally ordered and ate their meal and chatted for a long time, having quite a laugh together. As they laughed, they looked at each other for a long moment. Jack wasn't sure what was happening as his mind was going crazy. Vicky and Jack came closer and closer until their lips met – and then, at that exact moment, a sound wave blasted through the building shaking the ground beneath their feet. No one had a clue what was going on. The restaurant staff tried to rescue all the food they could, but most customers wanted to brace under a table in fear for their lives.

"Save the food! Save the food!" said one of the waiters.

"It's just food!" said one of the surprised customers, "but what is that sound?!"

"What's happening?" Vicky asked Jack.

"I'm not sure" said Jack, who was totally confused now.

Everyone looked over to the other side of the restaurant and saw a yellow glow flashing nearby that appeared to come from the alleyway next door.

"It's outside!" exclaimed Jack.

"Come on!" said Vicky, grabbing Jack's hand. Jack didn't want to go but it didn't look like he had any choice.

Many people from the restaurant went to the alleyway to see what the light was. What they saw was a *hollow*. It was large and it was surrounding the area. People were lining up at its edges to see what it was.

Jack and Vicky arrived in the area at the back of the line. It wasn't too busy, however; only the customers from the restaurant were there.

"What is it?" Vicky asked, with no idea.

"I don't know, Vick" said Jack, who was cautious about the thing, "Shouldn't we head back?"

"You're kidding, right?" Vicky asked incredulously. "Isn't this great! 2016, and we get to see something like this!"

"Well, it's not a bad thing to do" said Jack, diplomatically, "but we don't know what it is - it could be some kind of portal from another world."

Vicky stared at Jack if she thought he was some kind of nerd.

"What?" groaned Jack.

Then a big bang from the *hollow* burst down from the sky and crashed to the bottom. It seemed like something large had landed on its shimmering surface.

People were waiting for something or someone to step out of the *hollow*. Their expectations couldn't be higher.

"What landed?" Jack asked.

"I have no idea" Vicky said, now a little nervous as well.

Then, to their horror, a foot stepped out. But it was more a lean bony leg than a human leg. It had a brown reptilian skin with claw-like toenails. As the creature stepped out, the *hollow* disappeared and revealed a military shirt with shorts, covered by a flapping red cape. Its face was like some kind of Lizard; a Lizard that was mixed with other breeds from a crossed background. He was accompanied by a crew of creatures who looked the same. A few had green and blue reptilian skin and their capes were red, blue, and green.

These guys were tough looking and had come with BIG futuristic guns on their backs.

The people couldn't believe what was happening. They were shaking in their bones with excitement and wonder. Some filmed them on their phones and sent them up on social media.

The main creature bent his head forward to a man in front of him. The man was sweating and really nervous – more than a little bit scared. The creature just sniffed the man as the creature and his crew talked to each other in some king of alien language.

"Welcome to our planet!" said the man welcomely, "we come in peace, or is that something you guys don't say?"

The Alien sniffed at him again as people made way to let the Aliens through. Unbelievably, the Aliens all headed towards the back door of the Chickee's Chicken.

Everyone watched the creatures make their way inside the restaurant. Their jaws dropped. Some never had a single clue what they saw; some just wished this was a normal day. People these days had no idea what the galaxy was like. You tell people about the existence of aliens, but their friends say they're not real. Some people decided to leave the restaurant after they saw the aliens. Not in a terrified way – but because they wanted to share with the world that humans were not alone.

So, this was no normal day. It was a day people will remember because this was a day that everything would change about their knowledge of the universe. But then again, change may never happen, because sometimes people never understand.

******

The creatures sat at a table, to order at Chickee's Chicken. A waiter walked towards them to ask them for their orders. He was young, in his teens at best, so he must be one of the sons of the family.

22

"Can I get you anything…Lizards?" he asked, as he had no idea why they would come to his restaurant.

"Scrambled eggs, with raw beans" said one alien.

"Chicken legs," said the Leader.

"Me too!" said another one.

The waiter didn't mind what they wanted; he knew it was a strange experience to be taking an order from an alien.

"So…how are the stars, gentle men?" asked the waiter conversationally, as he looked at their uniforms. "Saving the galaxy, and all that?"

"Narrh" said one alien in a different language.

"Oh" said the waiter jumpily, "then I would…"

"I would prefer you kept your mouth to yourself, human" said the Leader, as he pulled out his big gun and pressed it to the waiter's chin. The waiter was shattering his teeth trying to apologise.

"Oi!" said the chef, with his wife and their two other sons walking towards the aliens, "If you want to point at a space gun at my son, you better point it at the food instead, sonny Boi!"

"You gonna get one soon you punk!" said the mother raising her fist.

The Leader looked at his crew as he wasn't sure what they were in for. The crew gave unsettling faces showing they thought they shouldn't get involved in human matters.

"Well?" said the father, "what is it going to be?"

The Leader looked at them directly. Then he said, "Fine," and put down his gun, "we'd better have something for an empty stomach rather than nothing."

The waiter boy walked away to his family. As they take the aliens order, the mother grabbed her son's ear and told him, "Didn't I tell you not to bother somebody's business if they are from outta space!"

Jack and Vicky had already come into the restaurant and sat at a nearby table. They were observing the aliens to try to work out why they were here. They were holding their menus to cover their faces as they pretended to order something.

Vicky was fascinated with the aliens. She never thought she would ever see aliens in person at all. Jack didn't really want to come, but he was curious about them too.

"What are we doing?" Jack asked as this was Vicky's idea.

"We need to work out why they're here" Vicky said, as she hid behind a menu page. "What if they're here to destroy the planet?"

"That's nonsense" said Jack. "Maybe they just wanted a space meal on their way across the galaxy."

"Please! As if that would be their idea" said Vicky believing that can't be true. "Listen, they're planning something, not just a free meal, but they're on to something."

Jack stared at Vicky as she kept on watching them, "Have you eaten anything?"

"Of course," she said normally. Jack wasn't sure that sticking around at the restaurant was going to help him get out of this craziness AND he still hadn't had a full meal.

4. Tracing the New Locals

Vicky and Jack watch over the aliens eating their meal. After they finish, the aliens walk out of the restaurant and head out to the alleyway they came from. They didn't take kindly to the waiters' politeness.

Vicky and Jack followed them sneakily. It was steamy and foggy. They kept close to the wall on their right where the buildings were more solid. Soon, however, the aliens took different turns away from the alleyway. They appeared in parts in the city that Vicky and Jack had never been before.

The Lizard aliens didn't know they were being followed. None of them turned to look behind them for a moment. It was very lucky for Vicky and Jack as the Lizards were much bigger than them; they might have been caught at any time.

"Man, these guys are dumb," Jack whispered to Vicky, only a few feet away from the aliens.

"Yeah," Vicky replied, "where you think they're going?"

"No idea," Jack answered, "maybe there's a place they're meant to be going."

"What place?"

"Some place; some space place".

Before they got back on track, they saw the Lizard aliens were at end of a crossroad and had entered the big city. Cars were screeching as the Leader stepped forward. The aliens simply ran across in front of the cars.

Vicky was running to catch up with them. "Hey!"

But before Vicky could catch up, Jack saw a car coming her way! He called out "Vick!" and pulled her back as the car drove past right in front of her. Jack worried about the safety of Vicky and was curious as to what action she would take to chase the aliens. Jack knew chasing aliens to be worth it but getting killed was another thing.

"I hate when you call me like that!" Vicky told him annoyed, upset with Jack.

"But…I saved your life, very much," Jack said, thinking Vicky was overreacting, and that he did indeed save her.

"But they are getting away!!" Vicky explained, who thought she must have lost them.

"Why are you so intense about this?" Jack asked her politely. "We were meant to have an actual date, Vick, we're not supposed to chase down alien creatures when they get lost."

"Well, who's fault was that then?" Vicky walked over the road and called out, "come on!!"

Jack should have gone home for his sake, but he followed her, knowing this day couldn't get more awkward, for either of them.

******

Vicky and Jack walked around the city to find the aliens. It was true they had lost the Lizard creatures, but they knew the aliens couldn't be far away. It was a normal traffic street they were on now.

"Great" Vicky called, "now what?"

Jack was scratching his chin to think, but what he saw was just the street's Plaza. Jack thought that if they wanted to go places where it would be hard to find them, the Plaza would be the best place to go.

"Hey Vick, I think we might have a trace."

They walked inside the Plaza. It was big, and the floors were white and black. The stores had windows on each side - it would be an expensive place for shopping. It also had a short hall, so they couldn't get enough of a view around them. Jack and Vicky looked in every store, and nothing seemed like the kind of place the aliens could escape to.

"Well, we took a wrong turn," Jack concluded, thinking he could get away that easy, but he still had the feeling Vicky was not done yet.

"Come on, Jack," Vicky told him, "we can't give up yet."

They kept on walking and turned left into another short hall, but they still couldn't see anything that looked likely. Then Jack saw a nerd store near him which was a bit torn up, and the title had some unusual lettering. Vicky walked up to Jack; they looked at each other and agreed they should enter. By now most humans would have decided to turn around and forget the whole thing ever happened. The world may get destroyed, but that would be someone else's problem. Jack and Vicki weren't like that. When they walked inside, they saw the place had been totally wrecked! Comic books were torn to shreds! It was a horrible experience for any fan to see!

Jack knelt as he looked at the mess around him. The comic book racks were half empty, there was hardly anything in them. Vicky was looking for something in the room, and soon spotted something.

"Jack!" Vicky called.

Jack turned and ran over to Vicky.

They could hardly believe it but there was secret door. They opened it and saw a small tunnel with brick walls. They look at each other locking eyes.

"You go," Vicky volunteered Jack.

"Me?!" Jack asked, like he was betrayed, "I didn't want to follow the aliens, did I?"

"Jack," said Vicky, trying to win him with her trust, "where do you ever find aliens coming to our planet, hide in a secret base inside a comic bookstore? Isn't that unreal or what?"

Jack thought about, but he still felt betrayed. They walked through the tunnel; it was quiet inside even though they were only feet away from the open plaza.

When they arrived at the end of the tunnel, they pushed open the iron door and they were in some basement. It wasn't too special; it had crates and all that stuff.

But, in addition to the crates, on the other side of the basement, was the group of aliens standing around in a circle. They were surrounding the Leader; he was kneeling and holding something.

"Soon, we will be able to bend them all together," said the Leader. He was holding a cork in his hand and writing some letters on the floor. It was a large circle with different symbols following a line that was going in a larger circle.

"Here, we'll summon the *hollows* together, at the same moment; we'll bring all the *hollows* to this place, all in one spot," the Leader continued. The aliens giggled as their master plan was as evil as it could get.

Then Jack sneezed and the aliens turned - snarling with teeth poking out. One alien walked over to Vicky and Jack and took them to the group.

"What purpose do you have here?" the Leader demanded.

"We…came to see the Movie," said Jack, scared of the fearsome creatures.

"Movie?" the Leader asked, as the other Lizard aliens talked among themselves.

"Well, that doesn't matter," Vicky said, taking a step towards the Leader, "we were following you from back where you had lunch."

"Yeah, thanks Vick." Jack mumbled, who wasn't going to talk about that. And he'll have a good chat about this later.

"Sir, they followed us!" said one of the crew.

"What do we do?" said another.

"Roast em?"

"Crunch em?"

"Oh, let's save them to eat later!"

"No!" called the Leader. "We'll do without any more meals tonight, gentlemen."

As the alien crew mourned, the Leader took out his big heavy gun from his back and pointed it right into Jack's and Vicky's faces.

"Ooook" Jack spoke shakily, "Mmmayyybe we could dissscussse this…".

"Maybe not." the Leader thought differently while smiling, "Like the old lady said, you should have stayed out of people's business, if they are from outta space."

Before the gun could fire, another *hollow* opened. It glowed bright and it swept the drawing from the floor into nothing.

"What's that?" said one of the crew men.

"Leave men!" the Leader demanded as they ran off, "we can't do it here! Not now!"

As the aliens run and escaped down another secret path, Vicky and Jack stayed to watch the *hollow* continuing to open.

As the *hollow* closed, they saw a man standing in front of them.

"Ah, hi" came a voice from a Librarian named Floyd, "I came here to chase after a missing *hollow*. You won't mind if I am a bit late?"

5. Back to School

Floyd arrived a bit earlier than he was supposed to. He and his new human encounters walked out of the comic shop and headed to the great halls of the plaza.

Vicky and Jack had no idea what just happened; they didn't know who this guy was or what business he had; but their best guess was that he might be from the future.

"I hope you don't mind if you saw something strange. Weird? Bizarre looking?" he asked Vicky and Jack, coming up close.

"Except you?" asked Jack, very curious about Floyd.

"Oh, I thought I might have bumped into someone who might have known if they saw a glowing yellow *hollow* besides mine?" said Floyd, disappointed, as he picked out his notebook and wrote down where he might find it next.

Vicky and Jack weren't sure if they should share their information with somebody who just popped up in front of their eyes. But they knew they saw stranger things today besides Floyd. "Wait!" said Vicky to get Floyd's attention "before you came, we saw some Reptilian-looking dudes who came here to try to make a…*hollow* you call it?".

Floyd looked blank, "What?" he asked, as he turned and walked right back to her. "What did they say?" and before Vicky could try to remember, "Come on, this is very important!"

"Hey!" said Jack, as he walked up to Floyd. "Back off, dude!"

"Every piece of information is important!" said Floyd to Jack; then looked back at Vicky. "What did they say?"

"They said, they were going to bend all the *hollows* together, at this place." said Vicky, who didn't understand at all. "I don't know what that means".

"Oh no," said Floyd, as his facial expression flicked into fear. "This is much worse than I thought. This year there wasn't meant to be some kind of *Hollow-Alimony*!"

"A what?" asked Jack curiously.

"A *Hollow-Alimony.*" Floyd turned to Jack, "You all won't know what I mean, would you?"

Then, before Jack spoke, Vicky got a ding from her phone, and she read something. "Oh God," she said, "they are on the other side of the street, two blocks away."

"Reptiles?" Floyd asks. "Sea Turtles, are they still a thing?"

"We don't have time," Vicky told Floyd urgently, "we need to get a cab straight away!"

Vicky and Jack ran out of the Plaza as quickly as they could. Floyd stopped as he wondered, "I don't want to be stupid but, what's a cab?"

******

They found the nearest cab and told the driver to head to Conifold Street. It drove to a skyscraper building where they arrived in time to see the Lizards terrorizing the citizens by roaring at them and laughing.

Vicky and the others wound their windows down as they watched the Lizards. "Oh my god!" said the taxi driver, "is that Lizards? Fighting back since the dinosaurs!"

"Sorry," Floyd tried to ask, "I'm still behind on which side of history this is?"

The Lizards stared back at Vicky and the others. They noticed they have still been followed.

"Boss!" said the alien that spotted them, "it's those puny humans!"

The Leader growled in frustration, "Then we shall dismiss them at once!" They all took out their guns and charged up their weapons. "Take aim!"

"Drive!" Jack called, and the driver stepped on it. The aliens blasted their laser guns but miss the humans and only partly hit the cab.

The Lizards then jumped on the cars around them.

"Go after them! Go!" Floyd said to the driver. He drove the cab as fast as he could.

35

The Lizards took turns as the cab chased after them. They all went in different directions and did not stop.

The cab took a harsh turn as the passengers held on and looked straight over at the Lizards.

The alien Lizards didn't have unique abilities, but they were pretty fast. The cab could catch up, but the Lizards took out their guns and tried to shoot them from all angles. They shot so many times that the passengers had to duck for cover.

"Cease fire! Cease fire!" Floyd thought desperately.

The Lizards led them into a tight traffic jam and the taxi driver tried to put on his brake. The brake held but the wheels spun. The taxi stopped before it could cause any road damage. Drivers around them beeped.

The taxi driver turned to his passengers, "No pay, get out" he yelled at them.

******

Floyd, Vicky, and Jack got out of the taxi and took a long walk through the city.

"Well, that went badly." Jack thought. He looked at Floyd as he folded his robe around himself. "Big question: who are you?"

"A bit complicated," said Floyd, who knew so much more than they did, "very complicated."

"Then who are you, then?" said Jack, as a simple question. "Your name?"

"Floyd." he revealed his identity. "I, uh…came here to find something that is very important."

Floyd looked at the small device he was given. "And I am in need of a hurry, so I hope you two could help me."

"Us?" asked Vicky and Jack at the same time.

"Well, I don't have anyone else, do I?" said Floyd obviously, as he had no other option. "I'm looking for some papers…."

"Papers?" asked Vicky.

"Normal papers with golden writing on it." Floyd said, describing them. "Anyway, if they bend all the *hollows* together, it will cause dire consequences across the universe, if we don't do something about it."

"Wow" said Jack, "that sounds bad."

"But we might know somebody who could help us with this sort of thing?" said Vicky.

"What, who?" asked Jack.

******

Heading back to Hula Collage wasn't normal in the school break. Jack, Vicky, and Floyd arrived in the hope of getting some help from somebody who might have the right knowledge of weird science of the unknown.

The hallways were empty with no students; lockers were closed and everything else was clean. But the teachers would still be around.

"Who did you think could help us?" asked Jack to Vicky.

"Because science is her speciality," Vicky said, "she knows much more than our normal teachers."

"Well, anyway," Floyd interrupted, "what I need is a big computer. I am thankful that I arrived in the right period."

"You say some weird stuff, you know that?" Vicky added.

"Yeah, like what's with the robe?" Jack asked.

Floyd stopped, offended by this questioning of his robe. "These robes are a special tradition where I'm from. It is very important to the one who wears it, wherever they go."

"Typical!" Vicky mumbled as she walked by.

Floyd looked back as she walked off and then looked at Jack, "What did I say?" Floyd asked confused.

"I have no idea" Jack tried to pretend. But he too couldn't care how Floyd dressed.

******

They arrive at a lab room. Tables were spread around the room with science equipment all over the place. Professor Rachial was working on an experiment with a microscope. She had been working on it for few weeks so that she could share the proof with the students when they came back.

"There you have it," she told herself as she was looking down at the atom. She didn't mind that no one was there.

"Ms Rachial!" said Vicky, as she came in with the others.

The teacher was startled and dropped her experiment, knocking over her microscope. All her breakthroughs were lost and forgotten, and no other scientist would discover them.

"What are you doing here Vicky!" she yelled at them. "Could you have seen I was busy?" She looked down to her broken microscope sadly, and then looked at Floyd running around a table, "And who is this lunatic?!"

"Ms Rachial," said Jack, "we need your help."

"Yeah?" she said, and it seemed that she was about to refuse, "I'll help you...on Monday!"

"Uh, excuse me," said Floyd, leaping over the table, "we have a crisis on our hands, and no one's got knowledge like yours."

Floyd froze and then thought. "Well, nobody has any relevant knowledge here that I can tell, but I heard you were the best there is."

"Really!" Ms Racial glared happily, proud of the comment. She took a deep breath, as calm as she could, and asked "What you need?"

"We need…your brain." said Floyd, uncomfortable as he must have got the wrong term. Jack and Vicky were so embarrassed.

Ms Racial focussed on the word Floyd said, "Hmmm, does it involve computer skills?"

"Well, that's where I was going with it" Floyd replied.

******

They later arrived at the big classroom with the rows of seats. Floyd took down the screen to start planning.

"What did he meant by my brain?!?!" said Ms Racial, about to smack the living day lights out of Floyd.

"That's not what he meant." said Vicky with a fake smile to make her teacher very comfortable. Then she turned to Floyd as he was kneeling down plugging in some wires. "Right, Floyd?"

"Yeah, sorry, got the wrong idea" said
Floyd, plugging the wires. He got up and walked
around the other side of the table.

"Ok," he said, "but I do need your help to
see if you could trace some Unknown lifeforms in
the area."

"I can't do that!" said Ms Racial, "Ask
Professor Miles."

"But he isn't here, is he?" asked Jack.

Rachial didn't say a word. "No," she finally
agreed sadly, "if only he could have taken the
afternoon shifts."

Then Floyd chuckled while he fiddled with
the wires. Then suddenly the screen from the white
board pops up with a picture of the Earth. It was so
clear; Vicky and Jack had never seen it up close
like that before. The Teacher tried to code their
location on the computer.

"Alright." She started to work, the Earth
zooming in to trace alien life forms. "So, it would
seem they came out of some kind of dimensional
portal."

As the image grew larger: "Hold on, it said
it's from another time?" Vicky and Jack looked at
each other with surprised looks.

"From the future! And…born on another
planet? This doesn't make sense!" said the
Teacher, as she took off her glasses.

Vicky and Jack looked at Floyd. Floyd felt chilly while they were looking; then he saw the situation very clearly.

"There!" he called out, pointing to a location on the screen, "there we'll find them! Come on, we can't lose them!"

Floyd, Vicky, and Jack ran off.

"Hey!" yelled Ms Racial, "who the heck was that guy?!" Then she looked back to her computer, "He has a remarkable brain, if I say so myself."

6. Apocalypse Day

It was in the centre of the city that the Lizard Aliens surrounded a footbridge, ready to summon the *hollows*. The Leader was making the same circle with the chalk he kept.

"Now is the time we'll summon the *hollows*" said the Leader, as he finished the final touches. "Right now! At this very moment!"

He looked over to one of his men who had a device that would help them summon the *hollows*. They were excited and smiled their reptilian smiles.

"Do it!" he demanded.

There, as the Lizard pressed a button on the strange device, a yellow glow formed, as people came to see what was happing. It would seem they thought it was a light show. The aliens were ready to hear the human comments. They watched on with grins on their faces.

Yellow light beams shot upwards from the chalk drawing into the sky. Where the beam hit the atmosphere, a whole bunch of creaky *hollows* emerged in different directions and split according to their own ways. The *hollows* had different colours from each other: blue, purple, pink, red. The colours represented the fact that they could be from different dimensions and totally different realities. They soon hit the ground and into the river, moving toward different parts of the city;

AND, as they landed, some other things started to walk out.

******

Floyd, Vicky, and Jack were in a different part of the city. They had no clue where the Lizards were, but they arrived at some interesting scenery that Floyd glared at.

"My!" he said. "I haven't seen anything like this in years!"

"What do you mean years?" Jack asked. "These sorts of things have always been a thing."

"Oh, and what you call that?" Floyd asked.

"Art?"

"Hmmm," Floyd thought, "sorry, this is so exciting and new to me." Floyd was absorbed in watching artists at work in a gallery-type building.

"Like everything else you saw today?" Vicky said.

Floyd had a big rule on traveling – not to divulge more than necessary. "Sorry," he said to them, "don't think you'll be getting anything out of me anymore."

Then a scream came a mile away.

"Do you hear that?" Floyd asked.

"The sound of terror?" Jack nodded.

"Let's go!" Floyd said, as they all ran toward the sound.

The artists were a bit disappointed about their new visitors running away; now they had no one to pay attention to they're crafty work - despicable!

******

People were fleeing the spot, and Floyd could see a not-so-cute flying creature that had wings like a bi-plane, three eyeballs in its forehead and spikes above its head.

"Floyd," said Vicky nervously, "I have seen some weird and strange stuff today, but do you have any idea what that is?"

"Oh!" said Floyd in surprise. "it's, um, a Keltrien from the Ramos Dimension."

"From what?" Jack said. This guy just kept spitting out stuff like that, and he was wearing slippers for crying out load.

But, speaking of spitting, the Keltrien was spitting out flowers from a flower shop he swooped into.

Jack glared at Vicky then at Floyd, "Do you have any idea how to stop it?"

"Ah, not really…" Floyd admitted, since, being a librarian, he had no experience in these things. The Keltrien spat everything out of its mouth and then charged straight into Floyd.

Suddenly Floyd was facing a creature that was about hundreds of years old and he feared he was going to get swallowed up. "I can do this!" he thought.

Floyd held on as the Keltrien snatched him up and took flight. It broke the glass roof as it splattered off the ground. Floyd and the creature were about three hundred feet above the building as the creature flew straight up. It flew far from the place where Jack and Vicky were standing.

They watched it rise hundreds of feet up, while they wondered how to chase it and catch up with Floyd.

It twisted and turned as it tried to get Floyd off. "Please! Stop!" Floyd called out.

It later flew around in the air like a Bi-Plane. It also sounded like a Bi-Plane that was crossed with a Bee.

It wasn't quite the fun Floyd was expecting. He could tell the Keltrien wanted to swallow him as it tried to suck him. Floyd was worried that if he couldn't keep holding on to it, he may fall and die.

The Keltrien passed by windows of tall buildings as people watched them, wondering what it was they saw out of their window.

The creature later dived down to the surface at hyper speed. It tried to hit cardboard signs and fly through the windows of the plazas. "People and Plazas" Floyd thought, "Gees."

As soon as Floyd reached a clear area that was wide without people, he finally let go of the silly and misfit creature. Floyd was at least twenty feet in the air when he rolled and landed on a stony path, relieved that the nightmare was over.

Vicky and Jack came over to see if he was OK. "Whatever you thought you saw," Floyd told them, embarrassed "please try to forget that happened."

As they stood there, they could see the *hollows* opening more and more, with unimaginable creatures appearing out of them.

A group of creatures that were the size of giants walked out with big hammers. They had one eye and their skin was dark purple.

Then a group of flying creatures like flies few out. They that had riders who were hunters with masks and hidden clothing.

Creepy mummy rag dolls moved like ghosts through a *hollow.* They had different pattens of colours on them. They were also whispering about something, as they tried to scare the people away-which was their goal by the way.

People screamed for their lives as they had no idea what was going on. *Hollows* opened, creatures came out, both stretching miles and miles across the city.

It was so crazy. Vicky, Jack, and Floyd looked up at the sky and saw creatures in many sizes coming to this world, invading it.

"Well, the world's doomed!" said Jack, trying to be funny.

"Why would someone plan a *hollow* tear in the universe?" Floyd asks himself, "Why couldn't they just invade 2078, when the Plague would have helped them?"

"What?" Jack asked Floyd.

"What?" Floyd responded, since he wanted Jack to be confused.

"What?"

"What?! What?!!"

"…" Jack stopped.

"So, if there's an invasion causing this to happen, why here?!" said Floyd in deep thought.

"Then what should we do?" asked Vicky, who thought this was very bad.

Floyd clicked his fingers, his thoughts popping from one angle to another, until something appeared at that moment. "I got it!"

Floyd grabbed out the little device LO-NO gave him. He pressed a button causing it to ring.

"What's that?" Jack asked Floyd.

"You'll see" Floyd said, glaring.

Then LO-NO appeared out of nowhere, so confused he couldn't stop looking all over the place.

"WHAT DID YOU DO?!?!" LO-NO said out of his mind. He instantly thought this was Floyd's fault (again).

"LO-NO" said Floyd, "a group of invaders, known as the Hertens, have caused a *Hollow-Alimony.*"

"GOOD GOD" LO-NO responded with a dizzy feeling.

"Is that a robot?" Vicky asked, as she was so blown away.

"Not now!" Floyd turned to Vicky, then looked back at LO-NO.

"I'M GONNA BE SICK…" LO-NO replied as he couldn't take it. So many creatures, so many bazar portals, all in the wrong time.

"LO-NO, you can't be sick." Floyd told him.

"I WANT TO BE."

Floyd sighed and looked straight at him, "We need to use a *Hollow-Diverter*".

"RIGHT ON!!" said LO-NO as he changed his mood and disappeared into thin air.

Floyd turned to Vicky and Jack as the world around them turned into mayhem. Creatures were destroying buildings and wrecking city property. "OK, if this is really happing, will it cause a break in the Time Stream and all that?" Floyd thought to himself.

"*Hollow-Diverter*?" Vicky asked him.

"It's a little something," Floyd explained - a bit.

Here he turned, and LO-NO arrived with two blasting-looking guns. They looked like shot guns but a bit futuristic and plugged into back-packs.

"What the heck is that?!" Vicky added.

LO-NO gave Floyd the Blasting Gun as he strapped the backpack on his back. *"Hollows-Diverters."*

'LET'S SAY THE FUTURE HAD A LITTLE PACKAGE TO DELIVER", LO-NO and Floyd were ready, saving the universe one *Hollow* at a time, "LETS SHOW THESE BAD EGGS WHAT WE'RE MADE OF!!!!"

******

The sky was so different from the normal blue sky with clouds; all you could see was all different colours changing in the sky. You wouldn't think you were on the same planet anymore.

What a *Hollow-Diverter* does is that it shoots out a laser that would return something to the dimension where it belongs.

LO-NO and Floyd ran over to a large street in the city. People were fleeing, and the creatures were causing chaos on the streets. When LO-NO and Floyd spotted the creatures, they shot their *Hollow-Diverters* at them, and, in the blink of an eye, the alien creatures disappeared back into their own reality.

Vicky and Jack tried to help people get out of the area and avoid the battle as much as possible.

A giant tried to walk towards LO-NO and Floyd as they keep beaming the laser on the creatures. They were so busy they did not notice the giant getting close.

"LO-NO!!" Floyd cried, "anytime now!!"

"YOU DEAL WITH YOUR AREA!!" LO-NO replied back, "I'M A LITTLE BUSY TOO!!!"

"Me Too!!!! Why not Deal with the giant first?!!"

"I'M NOT A BATTLE BOT!!!!".

Vicky saw an opportunity to help. She ran over and Jack saw her running towards the Giant. "VICKY!!!" Jack called out.

Vicky threw a letter box at the Giant's head. He looked back at her, and he was about to slam his clobber at her.

Then Jack did something quite useful on this adventure, as hopeless as he was; he kicked one of the giant's legs and told it, "Back off, eyeball!"

The Giant looked down at him in frustration and kicked Jack down like he was a doll. Vicky came to Jack, and they both looked at the giant. The giant was about to take swing at them, but LO-NO took a shot, and it was gone.

"SEE? GONE NOW!" LO-NO said, relieved.

Floyd ran towards them and said, "That's enough, we really have to find those Hertens, now!"

"IS ALL THIS TO DO WITH THE HOLLOW OPENING AT THE LIBARAY?" asked LO-NO.

"Must be," Floyd said, "but we need to find the papers first."

"Wait, the papers?" Jack said confused.

"What is this all about?" Vicky asked Floyd. "You are still not telling us?"

As they stood in silence, Floyd thought he should tell them anyway. "OK, me and LO-NO came from the far future, and one of these *hollows* opened and swallowed some of our most important papers in all existence!"

"What are these papers?" Vicky asked.

"I can't tell you," said Floyd, still blocking the truth, "I really can't tell you; people from my past will kill me if I do."

"OK," said Jack interrupting, "but can we at least stop the Lizards and the *hollows* first than get the papers?"

"We really can't" Floyd said as he really tried to tell them. "We can't lose more time; the papers would be off somewhere else."

Then he and LO-NO started to walk off.

"But we can't stop this without you!" Jack called out as hope was lost.

Floyd and LO-NO stopped. They thought it would be impossible and wrong to walk away. He and LO-NO look at each other, "HE IS RIGHT," LO-NO agreed, "WE HAVE TO PUT THINGS RIGHT."

Floyd knew how important those papers were; if they go, they would be lost forever! But fixing the *hollows* was also important.

He turned back to Jack and Vicky and said, "OK, but we need to find somewhere we could plan out our next move".

"I got that covered," said Vicky.

"Stop suggesting that place!!" Jack added.

7. Bad Taste

They were on their way to Hula College; it was quite a walk to get there from the city centre. Floyd and LO-NO still had their *Hollow-Diverters* which were starting to wear them down. They saw creatures wondering around and *Hollows* still opening. The sky was not normal anymore. It was a changing colour of flares that made the sky like a perpetual sunset above them.

"How could we possibly close them?" Vicky asked Floyd about the Hertens.

Floyd and LO-NO were getting tired. They were so tired in fact that they could not stop walking – one foot automatically followed another.

"It's tricky" Floyd replied, with a concern that showed he might not know how to stop them, "the *Hollows* have just opened, and that won't end there."

"When does it end?" Jack was afraid to ask.

"AS THE EARTH EXPLODES, IT WILL SCATTER ACROSS THE GALAXY TILL IT REACHES EVERY SINGLE PLANET AND EVERY WORLD, THEN EVERY DIMENSION WOULD COLLIDE!" LO-NO said with dramatic effect.

It made Jack's throat glop. "Well, let's just hope we get this over with, right?" He passed over to Vicky and said, "I'm sorry, for not believing you."

"You don't always have to believe me," she said petulantly.

"What?"

She glared back at him. "You could have stopped me at any time."

"But you pushed me to keep following you."

"I know," she said, knowing, "but I thought if something like this was happing, I just had to check it out."

Jack raised his chin, "Yeah, no worries."

******

As they arrived at the Hula College gates, they noticed that at the front of the school were the Hertens. They were scouting around as if they were checking something. There were only two of them; the rest of the fleet was somewhere else.

"Why are they here?" Vicky asked herself.

"Maybe you knew too much," Floyd said, standing next to her.

"SOMETHING BAD IS ABOUT TO GO DOWN" LO-NO thought, "I CAN FEEL IT!"

Floyd had no explanation for the illogical mind of a robot. Maybe it recoded itself to make thoughts and later modified them. Floyd had no clue how LO-NO could sense what about to happen. Floyd tried to ignore this as such a thought was not going to help *him* think.

Floyd was tinkering ideas through his head coming up with a plan. "Ok, is there a backway through the college?"

******

They entered in a back way to Hula College, reaching the same big classroom they were always fond of - or maybe Floyd really liked big screens in a massive classroom.

They tried to find where the Hertens might be, hoping to notice something and go and check it out. It was hard for Floyd and the others to trace a whole bunch of creatures and *Hollows* opening caused a problem for the computer to trace Hertens. It might break this sort of technology.

"Blast!" Floyd said in frustration, "I can't trace them through the scanner."

"What can we do?" Vicky asked wanting to help.

"If you tell the government to upgrade their system, it will help a lot!"

Jack leaned over to LO-NO and asked, "Does he normally get mad?"

"NO" LO-NO said in surprise, "HE NORAMLLY DOESN'T GET MAD, BUT

56

TODAY HAS BEEN A STRANGE DAY FOR ALL OF US."

"Same," Jack agreed.

"What can we do to help, Floyd?" Vicky tried very hard.

"I'm sorry" said Floyd deeply, "I really, really tried to find a way, but there's nothing I can do."

As they stood in shock and hopelessness, Floyd felt hopeless the most. He wanted to get those papers back and fix what the Hertens caused, but he was no superhero (as they were not a thing in this universe), so he couldn't stop something as big as this.

Then Ms Rachial entered the classroom, holding something in her hands, "OK" she said to them: it was a gun.

"Whoa!" said Jack, as Floyd stood up out of his chair.

"I will only tell you this once; listen and don't move!" Ms Rachial told them very directly.

"Rachial," Vicky said in shock, "are you working with the Hertens?"

"Well, isn't that pretty obvious?" she said with a little smirk they all saw on her face - it was pride. "With aliens coming out of nowhere, strange skies, and this man walking in here like he thought I was some kind of fool."

"I didn't say…," said Floyd.

"Zip it!" Ms Rachial demanded. "A group of Lizard blokes wanted you; two are waiting outside."

"Why?" Floyd wondered. They don't know who he was, he thought.

"They just…do." she said not trying to explain the situation. "I'll say they do describe me much more nicely."

"but I was…"

"Z.I.P IT!" she said as she pointed her gun for Floyd to go outside.

As Floyd started to walk out, the others began to follow but Ms Rachial pointed at them.

"Not you!!" she told them.

"But what are you going to do with us?" Jack asked his teacher. "We do still have exams and stuff, right?"

"Well, like you don't know?" she said, clueless. "They have other plans for all of you." She then looked at LO-NO. "Even you robot!!"

"HEY! I WASN'T BORN YESTERDAY MISS!" he said.

"It'll be OK guys" said Floyd, as he walked out of the classroom, and listened to what Ms Rachial told him.

******

Floyd walked out the front of the college and he could see the skies were getting worse; everything was colliding, and *Hollows* were still opening. Floyd had no choice but to go with the Hertens.

He saw two of them waiting for him. One nodded as he walked outside the school. The other growled at Floyd. Floyd just stood as he had no clue what to do. "So, you kill me or eat me? Or do you finish me off first than eat what's left?"

"No." said the big Lizard with a heavy grizzling voice. "I'm taking you with us so we can discuss some terms."

"Oh no," Floyd thought, "this had better not involve my resumé."

Floyd was lucky that he was just getting eaten for this. At least they understood what he was and not just a regular person who lived on the planet.

The Lizard showed him to a sleek black car that looked pretty evil for their taste; maybe too evil for their taste. Floyd hopped in the back with seats that were all red; then the Lizard drove off without his friend.

******

Floyd arrived at an Asian Restaurant a few miles away. It had a massive room with red lanterns all over the place.

The people and the waiters were too scared to serve the Hertens. The Hertens were eating their dinner to feast and reward themselves. They were chewing chicken, noodles, and other dishes in pots as big as they were. They were enjoying themselves like they won a trip to a holiday island.

Hertens weren't the greediest creatures in the galaxy; they were designed to eat a large amount of delicious food, as disgusting as they were. It was part of their biology.

Floyd entered the room with the one Herten who took him in. He felt he was part of an uninvited party that no one told him about.

The Leader spotted him first, then the others followed his gaze. "Ahh!" said the Leader in the centre of the table. "Isn't that the Librarian!"

"Well, I prefer the name Floyd" as relaxed possible under the circumstances. Floyd was not afraid to meet somebody that looked imposing; but he knew not to show his response to their foulness to one who wanted to discuss bushiness.

"Well, Floyd," said the Leader very generously. He leaned closer across the table, "I had a hunch you might arrive."

"How did you know that?" Floyd asked, wondering if they could tell the future.

"We saw that you took all the creatures back where they came from."

"Blast, maybe that wasn't the best option to do yet," Floyd told himself, annoyed. "Why are you trying to break all of reality?" he asked petulantly.

They didn't say anything but stared with a more serious look.

"Come now," said the Leader, "we only wanted to bring the others so they could rip this planet to shreds."

"By now you would understand that if you damage the planet in this timestream, you won't only break it, you'll break the entire universe, like the big bang but with a bigger bang!" Floyd called out very effectively. "Why do it? I know you would be busted in your own time stream, but this world isn't advanced."

"Their whole entire reality isn't enough." said one of the Lizard aliens in rage. "We wanted all the creatures to take their share! Including us!"

"Thank you," said the Leader to his crewman. Turning again to Floyd, "I brought you here for one, simple reason."

"Yeah?" Floyd asked in case he was bluffing, "and what is that?"

"The papers!" the Leader said truthfully. "I could take you where the papers are if you promise to leave us alone."

Floyd would not buy that, but it seemed so true, he couldn't deny it. "Really?" he asked as he thought the Leader was still bluffing.

"Indeed!" said the Leader. "I could take you where they went, in another *Hollow*, into another dimension. I could help you."

Floyd had everything he needed, but he knew that breaking the fabric of this world would be even more damaging than losing the papers.

"but…" he said refusing, "you are still breaking reality!"

The Leader clicked his fingers. Walking out of the kitchen was Jack and Vicky. Their hands were bound, and apples were stuck in their mouths. The same Herten from the college was taking them to their table.

"I brought them for this kind of occasion." said the Leader, starting to appear more imposing than ever. The other Hertens laughed about their evil plan. "This is what I mean, get what you can or get lost."

Then Floyd thought about one last thing, "What about LO-NO?" he asked the Leader.

The Leader smirked and spoke, "Well, I sent my one of my men to take him to pieces."

Floyd raised his eyes in redness and wanted to try to fight him, but two of the Hertens grabbed hold of him. "OK, you have gone waaay too far now!"

"Well, then," said the Leader, as a blue *Hollow* appeared on the side near Jack and Vicky, "I give you one chance. Come with me as I take you to the papers and you'll be off like this never happened, or you could rescue your new friends and fix their universe. Your choice."

The Herten threw Vicky and Jack into the *Hollow*, as they screamed.

Floyd couldn't make up his mind. He knew if he went with the Lizard to get the papers it could be totally fine, but then they killed the one robot who kept him on track. Floyd chose quickly. He chose Vicky and Jack as he jumped into the blue *Hollow*.

The aliens laughed, "Then you chose them for your quest!" said the Leader.

"Go Librarian!" said one of the crewmen teasing, "go and save your universe!"

8. Inside the Hollow

Floyd arrived face down into the snow. He looked back at the *Hollow* behind him as it was closing. His only opportunity to reach the papers was gone, but with a more worthy cost.

He saw his two friends Vicky and Jack on the snow, still with their hands tied and apples in their mouths. Floyd ran over and freed them.

It was a breezy snow on a hill and the sky was dark. As Floyd freed his friends, and they all got up and looked over the area.

"We're lost!" Jack said to Floyd.

"Well…" Floyd started as he looked around him; he wasn't an expert on interstellar places, but he was sure he had no clue where they were. "I'm not entirely sure."

"Then we're stuck!" Jack said in outrage.

"Are you sure rescuing us was the best option?" Vicky asked Floyd in the cold.

"Well, it was the best course of action," Floyd replied, "if it means I wasn't thinking this through properly, and it had to be a fast decision."

"What was your best option?" Vicky asked Floyd curiously.

"Neither" he responded, "but I did come after you."

"Thanks," Jack said critically, "that's what they wanted you to do, isn't it?"

"Well, maybe," Floyd replied carefully, "but I thought I might go with them if they didn't kill LO-NO."

"The robot?" Jack said in shock. "If they kept him alive, you would have gone with them?"

"Well, I'm not entirely sure." Floyd tried to back away, "I might have still rescued you. By the way, doesn't anyone know we're trapped in a *Hollow* and the whole of existence is at stake!"

While Floyd and Jack were arguing, Vicky was looking around and she noticed something over the snowy hill. "Guys! Up here!" Jack and Floyd ran up and saw what Vicky saw in the distance. "You see that?"

"It's a village!" Jack said with hope.

"Oh, dear!" replied Floyd.

"What?" Vicky asked.

"We might be somewhere that could make us breakfast…." Floyd said in a worry. "The bad way of breakfast."

"What's the bad way?" Jack asked.

Floyd thought he would leave the problems for later, "Come on" he said as they slid down towards the village.

******

It seemed, as they arrived, that everything was about 20 metres taller than they were. It was like Christmas town. The place was made of wood, lights, and poles, with old fashioned windows.

"Where the heck are we?" Jack asked as he had no idea what this place was. This didn't freak them out, not even Floyd; he was pleased to bump into such a place as this - he was at home in a way.

"Well, it's complicated," Floyd explained.

"Yeah, we get the picture," said Vicky, who has heard that many times, "but where are we? Not what this place is?"

"Just say it's like everything you might know about your reality, but stranger." Floyd tried to tell Jack and Vicky more about this world than he knew, without making them think he was making stuff up or making their heads explode. This was no easy matter, as the universe was even worse than anyone realised.

Then someone came out of a door; it had a normal body, but the head…it was a dog. And I mean an actual dog.

As it walked by it looked at the small humans, wasn't impressed, and just left them alone. Vicky and Jack couldn't tell what happened, but they were speechless, and their expressions couldn't change for hours afterwards.

"Oooook" said Jack struggling to speak.

They walked into the door the dog-man-thing came out of. It was a bar. The dog men were the same size as the town – all around 20 metres tall. It was so strange; the humans were doll sized, so not noticed.

"So, Floyd," Vicky asked, "how do we get out of here?"

"Well, we just find another *Hollow* like no other" said Floyd simply.

"Then open one!" Jack pleaded.

"If I could, if LO-NO was still alive, he could help us get out of any mess we were in." Floyd said. It was a problem, and he needed a plan A or B -and fast. "We need a new strategy. We need to get close to a nearby *Hollow*, so we can catch it whenever it hits."

"But how could we possibly do that?" Vicky asked as it sounded impossible.

Floyd had no idea. Even in the most hopeful of times, it would be hard to come up with a plan.

"We ask the locals" Floyd speculated.

"You're not serious," Jack said, "those Dog-man-things?"

"I say those Dog-man-things won't know what you are," Floyd said defending them, "but keep an eye out, or they might cook you up if we don't leave soon."

Floyd walked past as Vicky and Jack stood there. "What?!" said Vicky and Jack together.

Floyd climbed up onto a stool and upwards onto the bench until he stood in front of a Bulldog.

"Uh, excuse me," Floyd said pertly, as the Bulldog's head bent down to his height, "I wonder if you know any nearby *Hollows* that are opening, do you?"

"Oi" The Dog spoke deeply, "I say there will be one in several minutes."

"Really?" Floyd said interested. His friends were trying to climb up while Floyd was busy talking.

"Ya" the Dog spoke, "I wouldn't say it would be possible to find it tonight my friend, it will be gone soon."

"Oh!" said Floyd. This sounded bleak to Floyd. He would miss it very soon, but his mind kept thinking there had to be a way to reach it.

******

Floyd, Vicky, and Jack entered through the kitchen door. A Scottish-Terrier who was wearing a chef outfit was making pizza in the pizza oven. It would seem Floyd had another genius plan in mind.

"So, what's your plan?" Vicky asked Floyd, afraid to find out....

"I thought I could possibly open up the *Hollow* like the Herntens did" Floyd thought.

Then Jack had it, "The chalk! But that would mean opening more of them! You'll break even more of the Time-continuum!"

"I'll figure that out" said Floyd, knowing he would find a way to fix it afterwards.

"But how can we come up with that?" Vicky asked, as it was so important.

"I…'ll come up with that" Floyd said, even though he didn't know how yet.

The Dog walked away as the pizza was cooking. Floyd stared at the oven as Jack and Vicky looked at him and at the oven.

"We're doing it in there?!" Jack asked.

Then Floyd thought he might have had the most insane idea in his head.

"You're not serious!" said Vicky. She had had quite a day, and seen things she couldn't believe, but this was too crazy. Even for Floyd.

"Alright." said Floyd who had settled on what he was about to do. "If we do it inside, like in a pie, without being cooked, a *Hollow*, maybe even a bigger one, could possibly take us where we need to go."

There Vicky and Jack said together, "Your nuts!"

"Well maybe," said Floyd, who thought it was not a bad idea, "but we've got to try, right? With positive attitude." Vicky and Jack looked gutted.

******

They jumped inside a pie without the Dog Chef noticing. The Dog put the pie inside the oven as it was heating up. There Vicky and Jack drew on the bottom of the pie with chalk, while Floyd held the same device that LO-NO gave him back in the Library.

"You got it ready?" Floyd asked them without rushing them.

"Not as much as if you could cool down the heat!" Vicky responded while they all sweated in there.

The pie was lighting up with the air all steamy; they couldn't feel the bottom of the oven as the heat drove them out of their comfort zone.

"This was a dumb plan of yours!" Jack told Floyd, with a lot of sweat on his face. "I'm going to get cooked by dogs because of this."

"Well, it's better than Big Bang Two!" Floyd replied.

The oven was getting even warmer inside. They were all boiling and couldn't take more heat. The drawing was vanishing through the steam.

"It's fading!" Jack told Floyd.

"You almost have it!" Floyd said, to keep them on track. They were so close to the upcoming *Hollow*; it was showing up on the scanner.

Soon the Dogman noticed something was going on inside the pie. He couldn't pin-point what it was.

Then as Vicky and Jack got the drawing completed, Floyd pressed the button to summon another wave of *Hollows*. It was all going on inside the pie, but it was trying to reach outwards, and couldn't reach further than inside the oven.

"What you do?" Vicky said to Floyd.

"I thought that now we're in two *Hollows* stuck together, they won't be able to spread in the oven," said Floyd, proud that his master plan was working so far.

"Oh, I love this guy!" Jack fed back.

"If the *Hollows* combined together, we might have our next destination." Floyd continued.

"And that is?"

"We head where all the *Hollows* go," Floyd said wisely, "the web between the *Hollows*".

Then as Floyd finished, a big light blinded them as it all turned to white, then into blackness.

9. Web of *Hollows*

After a dangerous attempt, Floyd, Jack, and Vicky summon the *hollows* inside a pie in an oven. This was a terrible plan; it still was, but it worked.

They arrived in some tunnel, mysterious and unknown. As they got out, they walked in an area with very tall purple mountain walls. There was also shinney crystals that glowed from above, that helped them see. They could also make out the sky at the very top in the darkness.

Soon they could see something close ahead, with blue light.

"What is it?" Vicky asked, as they walked closer.

"I don't know" Floyd said. The first time on their adventure, he had no idea what would lie in front of him; he hadn't been anywhere like this in his lifetime. But this also made him curious about what to expect.

They walked further as they wanted to see what was out there. They were all curious about what was there, and none of them knew where they were - it was all a big mystery.

They walked to a different area and saw a blue light shining out of a big hole. The place still had mountain walls and crystals and there were spiky cliffs coming out of the ground and into the hole.

Floyd ran over to the big hole and saw that it would seem the hole never stopped going down. Vicky and Jack thought it would be a lot safer if they walked on the other side.

"What is it?" Jack asked Floyd as he looked down.

Floyd learned a truth as he stared deep down, "I think we have found the source of all the *Hollows.*"

"Well, done!" said the Herten's Leader as he stood on the spiky clefts with his men.

Jack and Vicky jumped, as they never thought the Hertens would be here. "How did you get here?" Jack asked.

"Yeah," Vicky told them, "weren't you meant to be destroying our planet?!"

"We thought you may have few more tricks up that Librarian sleeve, so we thought we may come here just in case." said the Leader with pleasure. "Did you think I would be fooled if you tried escape, and you would come walking in here to stop us?"

"No…" said Floyd as he wasn't thinking clearly, "but can we at least take a break?"

"No!" the Leader roared at them, as his men walked around the cave. "You have made a breakthrough, I give you that, but when it comes to me and my friends, you won't survive!"

There he swung across and slammed Floyd into some crystal rocks behind them. Floyd fell downwards into the hole.

Vicky and Jack turned behind them and looked down to where Floyd fell. "Floyd!" Vicky called out.

But then Jack pointed at Vicky's shoulders. "Vicky!' he cried as she turned. Two of the crewmen were coming up with sprint speed. "We should get out of here!"

The Hertens fire their purple lasers, blasting out but missing Jack and Vicky, as the crystals got destroyed and shattered.

Vicky and Jack ran in terror as everything was more frightening now. The Lizards weren't going to give a break.

They rolled on the ground away from where the Hertens were searching for them, "Hey you!" one of the Hertens called another, "See if you can check over that way."

The Lizards crawled over the area, with their big guns in their hands as they sniffed and looked over at the crystals. Jack and Vicky hid behind crystals, which were thankfully not see through.

Jack and Vicky popped their heads out as the Lizards kept searching. They wondered if they should get out of there when they have the chance.

"Found Them!" said one of the Hertens at their faces.

Jack and Vicky backed away as the Herten walked towards them, smiling greedily as it licked it lips. "You Mine!" it said. "My Boss will be proud, and he'll give me the delightful meal I deserve!"

"Wh-hat you mean?" Jack asked shakily.

The Lizard smiled. "It means I get all the credit!" as the Lizard punched Jack who accidentally pushed Vicky on the ground.

Vicky turned as Jack had a rough bump on the floor. The Herten blinked as Jack slowly crept up.

Vicky grabbed Jack's arm "Come on, Jack!" she called out, and they rushed towards the tunnels before the Hertens could trace their steps.

******

Inside the tunnel, Vicky and Jack arrived at another big cave, and they could again see the sky above them.

Vicky felt she betrayed Floyd. She had previously thought she could take on anything. Now, she didn't know anymore. "What should we do?!" she asked Jack.

Jack didn't know. He felt like he also let everyone down. He feared what the Hertens might do next if they ever returned. But he didn't feel bad for what he stood for all day; he wasn't going to let Vicky, Floyd, or the entire universe down.

"We go back!" he said with bravery and courage.

"Go back?!" Vicky asked, "but we'll die!"

This was pretty obvious to Jack too, but he knew there was something greater they had to do. "We'll fight them off as hard as we can! Floyd needs our help!"

******

Floyd was hit badly from the crash; he landed with a rock on his back. The Herten Leader stood up. He was strong, stronger than Floyd, and he thought he won the fight from a wimpy human.

"You lost Librarian," he laughed as Floyd thought it wasn't fair, "you have no plan to stop this; you know it well."

Then as the Leader was chatting away, Floyd looked for something on the Leader that could help. Floyd saw a device, a pretty bad device, the Lizard had on him.

Floyd then took the most violent action he had ever done - he kicked the Leader's knee and then kicked again to the small device, that stung the Leader to the ground.

Floyd got up and jumped onto a clear surface attached to the wall, and he saw something so clear above. The missing papers!! They were dangling on a spike without harm, "Thank the Heavens" he said in relief.

******

Jack and Vicky crept their way back as they re-traced their steps. They stopped as they spotted the same two Hertens searching for them.

Vicky and Jack ducked their heads below a rock as they noticed the Hertens were debating, debating?!

"Why did you let them go?" said the green caped Herten who sounded annoyed.

The other one snarled. "They slipped out of my grasp!" said the blue caped Herten.

Vicky and Jack watched what was unfolding in case it was important.

The Green Herten snarled back as he looked away from his buddy. "I knew we shouldn't let those puny humans off the food chain." he thought angrily. "I could sweep and smell…Wait!" he called out, "can you smell that?"

"Yeah," the other Herten replied as he also sniffed around Jack and Vicky's direction, "Why does it smell so familiar?"

"Who cares, at least it's worth every bite!" the Herten said as he charged his gun. But when the Hertens arrived at Jack and Vicky's spot, the humans were gone!

******

Jack and Vicky sneakily headed back to the cave where the light was, but a Herten was guarding the entrance just in case they came back. He wasn't very smart as Jack found it easy to knock him out with a rock.

Jack smiled and laughed, "I can't believe I did that!"

Then, two other Hertens spotted them from either side of the cave, aiming their guns at them. Vicky took Jack's hand and said, "Maybe that could wait, don't you think?"

******

Floyd jumped on the spiky rocks to get away from the Leader. There weren't many rocks that could be jumped on, and the surfaces were very small so that he could easily fall.

Floyd was just happy that he could keep the Leader distracted while he hopefully got his hands on the papers. Floyd found himself feeling more joyful at having found the papers, than in terror at running from the Leader.

"You won't get away from me, little man!" the Leader called rudely.

"Oh yes, I will!" Floyd called.

But the Leader took a big and mighty jump over to Floyd and slid towards the edge of a rock for Floyd to face his doom.

******

Jack and Vicky were running away till four of the Herten crewmen blocked them. Then they were huddled together with no escape.

The Lizards were charging their guns to fire. Jack and Vicky went the other way as lasers blasted past them and they jumped over to a small area of rocks where the blasts were blocked.

Vicky and Jack realized that Floyd gave Vicky the device that summoned the *hollows.* Vicky stared at it as if she had an idea; Jack shook his head, "No."

"But what if we could try to use it on them?" Vicky thought. "There has to be a button where it could take them back to their world?"

Jack studied the device; it was hard to tell what to press. There was a yellow button that gave him the feeling that was the right one to press. Jack turned around for a moment and saw that same button on the Lizard's shoulders.

"If we hit one of those big yellow buttons, I think it would take them back to where they came from." Jack said to Vicky, who agreed totally.

They ran out to race over to the Lizards. Vicky saw one next to her, and as she tapped the yellow button on the Lizard's shoulder, the Lizard alien was gone.

Two Lizards were charging at them as Jack grabbed and threw two stones at their yellow buttons and they disappeared.

Then the last one aimed his gun at Jack and started shooting. Jack ducked down as he slid towards the alien, then he tapped the alien, and it was gone.

Jack got back up and saw Vicky who was so amazed, "Jack, that was so cool!" then she hugged him.

Jack blushed, "Well, you were pretty amazing too!"

Floyd tried to get up, but the Leader put his foot on him to not let him move. "I won't let you stop what we're doing!" the Leader yelled.

Floyd tried to move around, until he could jump onto the Leader and start them fighting each other on the ground.

Vicky and Jack tried to figure out which button to press from Floyd's device. "It's this one" Vicky decided.

"Wait!" Jack told her, "remember, if you press the wrong one, we'll end up somewhere else."

"Then which one are we supposed to press?" Vicky asked him tensely.

Jack was looking at the buttons carefully and pointed at the button he thought they should press. Vicky looked at Jack in the hope they got the right one.

She pressed the button. Vicky and Jack couldn't tell if they pressed the wrong button or what. But then the lights were doing something. It would seem they were pulling them back into the hole somehow.

The Herten Leader knelt up and called out, "The end is here! Everything is now gone!" as he closed his eyes.

Floyd thought of a good idea, as the Leader noticed something was up. "Wait, something is happening!" he said.

Floyd pushed the Leader into the light.

Floyd had his left hand on the surface, with no way to get up. Then somehow, something was happening around him. Lights maybe, he thought, then he suddenly appeared to his friends.

"Floyd!" Vicky called out, "we did it!"

"Wait, uh," Floyd asked confused, "how did I get up here?"

Vicky and Jack looked at each other for a moment, "We managed to work out how to use the device!"

There Vicky kissed Jack right away after his finished telling Floyd.

Floyd was grossed out at seeing them, "Ugh!" he said as he walked off.

10. A New Beginning to Be Written

After saving the universe and fixing all of the *hollows*, Floyd took Jack and Vicky back to Earth, back to where they had their Twelve O'clock lunch.

It was Ten Past Four on the same day; sundown was coming up. This was the same time the *hollows* returned to where they came from. The *hollows* were gone, and people calmed down as if they thought nothing ever happened.

"It really happened," said Vicky, as the day was getting quiet, "all the things we saw, did really happen."

"Well not for everyone," said Floyd indicating that was a good thing.

Vicky and Jack turned to Floyd as he was holding the piles of papers.

"Are you going?" Vicky asked.

"Afraid so;" Floyd said, "have to put them back, fix up LO-NO, buy repairs, tell everyone that it was fully my fault and my responsibility."

"You're so strange sometimes," Vicky added as Floyd chatted away.

Jack took a step further and asked, "Are we ever going to see you again?"

Floyd said solemnly, "Probably not, I have a big responsibility."

"Then this is the last time," Vicky said, who thought they had made a new friend.

They all stood in silence. Then Floyd felt a bit uncomfortable for a moment. "Don't mind me, I think I shall be off," he said as he took his device out.

"Floyd…," said Jack. Floyd turned before he teleported away, "Good luck".

Floyd nodded and took off as he teleported away. The mysterious stranger disappeared in front of them, leaving the two humans alone.

******

Quite some time flew by as Floyd was busy taking his time to fix the Library. He was carefully putting all the papers back in all their rightful books.

It took a whole lot of work to do.

Floyd also designed a rebuild of his annoying robot LO-NO. LO-NO took a bad beating from the Hertens, and Floyd had to put him together part by part.

As much Floyd tried to put LO-NO together, LO-NO wasn't quite back to normal; he had glitches most of the time.

It was going to take Floyd a while to get LO-NO back and running properly, so he decided to also build another robot called LO-YO. LO-YO helped him out a bit and fixed LO-NO on his feet.

Floyd was right back at home, relaxing, using more Piano lessons. He was fine then playing the piano.

But one day he was walking down in the library as he was reading something. He remembered when he had such an adventure, where he met up with two young people, searching for unknown lifeforms, taking down creatures from other worlds, making a getaway into another dimension inside a pie. He remembered all that in one single day, the adventure, the joy, the friendship. All of it. he remembered it all.
He sat quite for some time and decided to do something; the library can't be all there is. There must be something he must do in his lifetime. He had nothing good to do, but to seek new adventures.

"LO-YO!" he called out to his new robot. The robot ran fast towards the Librarian as he crashed into some pile of books, "YES, SIR?"

"I want to give you a job," Floyd told him directly, "a very important job."

"WHAT IS IT?" the robot asked very reasonably.

"I want you to look after the Library, guard the books, fix up LO-NO, teach him how to walk and all that, and go further into the unknown" as Floyd ran up the stairs.

"BUT THAT IS YOUR DUTY, IS IT NOT?" LO-YO said accusingly.

"I'm not leaving." Floyd said to it. "I'm going to see what's out there! Into the wild, into the abyss! I'm going to explore the cosmos more than anyone before!"

******

Floyd was planning to stay in the Library, but he wanted LO-YO to take up his work. Floyd re-programmed him before left, so the library was just a two-robot job now, meaning no offence towards the robots.

Floyd felt what it was like to be human again. It had been so long since he felt that.
He couldn't tell where to go, space was so massive to explore. The stars and beyond. Floyd wanted to see what he could do, study, help, whatever the task was, he'd do it.

Before Floyd could start his very first own adventure, he thought he might bring his new best friends: Vicky and Jack. He thought they could tag along on whatever adventure he may take them.

He arrived at a laundry room, where the walls were full of tech, and he wasn't sure where he was. "Hello?" he called out as he crashed into some baskets, "is anyone home?"

A door opened, and a young man appeared. He had short black curly hair and he was around in his late teen years.

"Who are you?" he said to Floyd. "Why are you in my laundry?"

"Oh" said Floyd as he wasn't trying to intrude, "I was finding a way in. Do you know where I could find Jack and Vicky, do you?"

"Sorry," said the kid, "I can't."

"Why not?" the Librarian asked.

"Because Jack was my grandfather" said the boy, "I'm his grandson."

There Floyd realized how time did go fast when you're drifting in space.

THE END*?*